Gg Hh Ii Jj Kk Ll Mm

Uu Vv Ww Xx Yy Zz

Dear Parent,

The My First Steps to Reading® series is based on a teaching activity that helps children learn to recognize letters and their sounds. The use of predictable language patterns and repetition of familiar words will also help your child build a basic sight vocabulary. Your child will enjoy watching the characters in the books place imaginative objects in "letter boxes." You and your child can even create and fill your own letter box, using stuffed animals, cut-out pictures, or other objects beginning with the same letter. The things you can do together are limited only by your imagination. Learning letters will be fun—the first important step on the road to reading.

The Editors

My "t" Book

(Blends are included in this book.)

written by Jane Belk Moncure

illustrated by Colin King

Little  had a box.

"I will find things that begin
with my 't' sound," he said.

"I will put them into
my sound  box."

"I like toys.
I will look for toys."

Little  found a toy train

on a train track.

Did he put the toy train and
the track into his box? He did.

Little 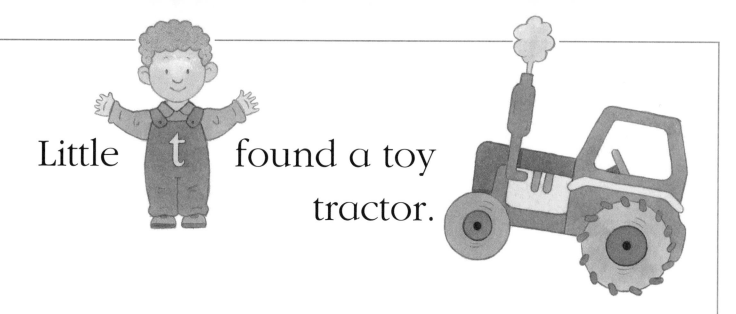 found a toy tractor.

Did he put the toy tractor into the box with the toy train and the track?

He did.

Then Little  found a truck.

He drove that truck up, up, up

a tall mountain.

He drove to the top,
the very tip-top!

At the top of the tall mountain,
he found two turtles.

Did he put the two
turtles into his box?
He did.

Then he found

a toad.

Did he put the
toad into the box?
He did.

Now the box was so full that he could not see over the top.

He tripped.

He tumbled down,

down,

down the mountain.

He tumbled into a turkey.

Turkey feathers flew!

So Little t made a
turkey-feather hat.

He and the turkey danced together.

Little  found a tambourine.

He tapped the tambourine,

"Tap, tap, tap.
Tap, tap, tap."

Little  t , the turkey,

and the toad
danced some more.

Then he put all of
his things into the box.

Suddenly, Little  heard a
terrific noise!

He ran . . .

into a   tent.

When he looked out, he saw a

tiger.

The tiger opened its mouth.
There were many

teeth

in the tiger's mouth.

"I have a loose tooth," said the tiger.
"Please pull out my tooth."

So Little  pulled out the tooth.

"Thank you," said the tiger.

Then Little  and the tiger went inside the tent.

They played with all the toys in the box.

tambourine

toad

truck

tractor

turkey

tent

two turtles

tiger

train

train track

They had a terrific time!

Can you read these words
with Little t ?

telephone

tulip

tray

tricycle

toe

tree

tomato

toothbrush

television

tie

table

top

taco

teapot

29

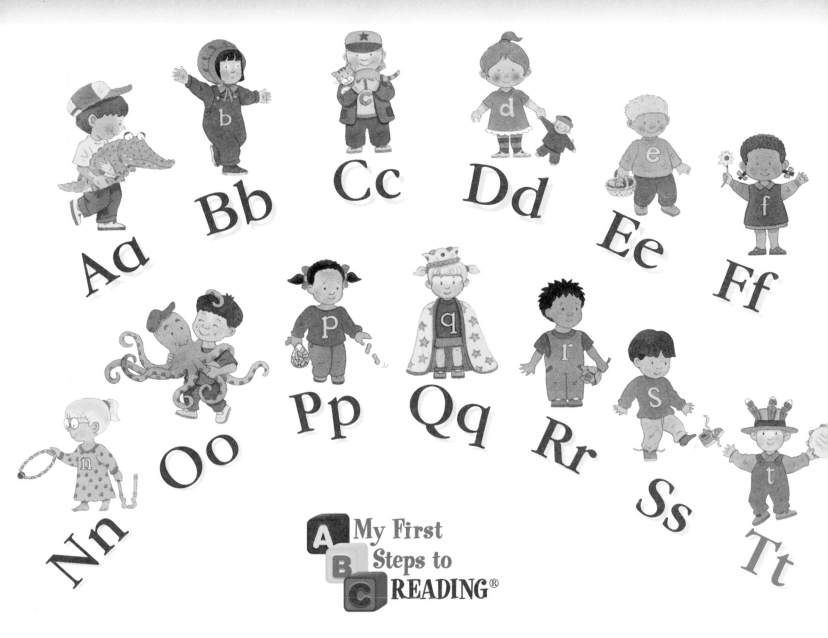

Aa Bb Cc Dd Ee Ff

Nn Oo Pp Qq Rr Ss Tt

My First
Steps to
READING®